Bree Finds a Friend

To Johanna, who knows how to be a friend
—Mike Huber

To Alina, my honest little firecracker, who keeps me on my toes
—Joseph Cowman

Published by Redleaf Lane
An imprint of Redleaf Press
10 Yorkton Court
Saint Paul, MN 55117
www.RedleafLane.org

First edition 2014
Book jacket and interior page design by Jim Handrigan
Main body text set in Billy
Typeface provided by MyFonts

Manufactured in Canada
20 19 18 17 16 15 14 13   1 2 3 4 5 6 7 8

Library of Congress Control Number: 2013939330

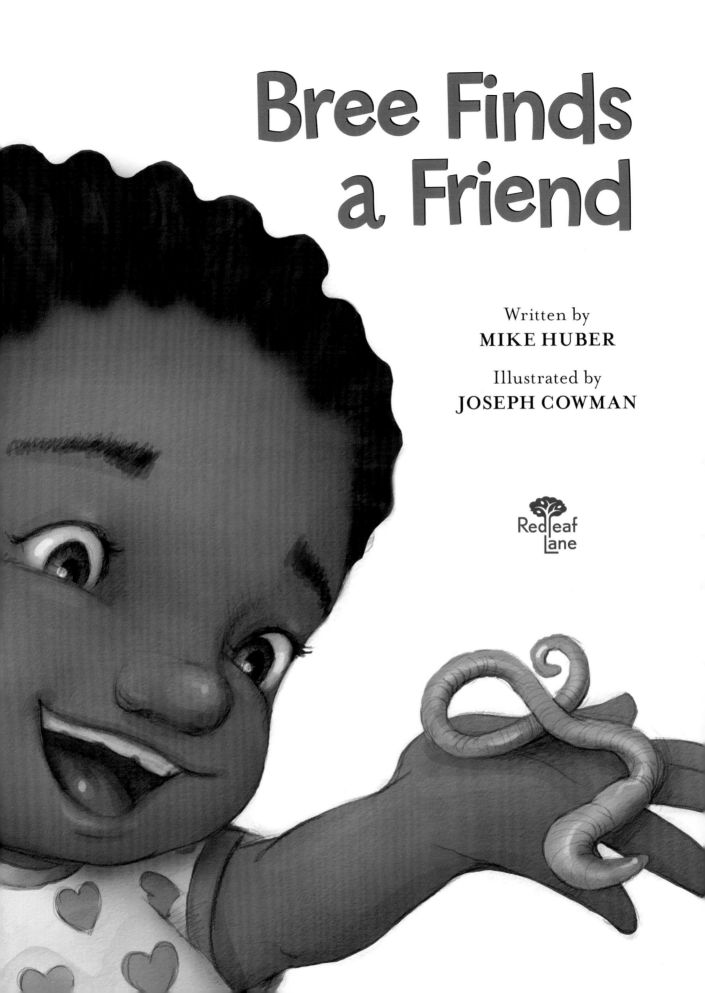

Bree Finds a Friend

Written by
MIKE HUBER

Illustrated by
JOSEPH COWMAN

Redleaf Lane

It was outside time. Michi and Jayden were playing chase. They always played chase together, because they were friends.

Rita and Curtis were playing ice cream shop.

Johanna and Maude were doing the monkey bars.
They were all friends too, like Michi and Jayden.

Bree was playing by herself. She was digging near the garden, pretending to plant blueberries. That's when she saw something.

"I found a worm!" Bree held the worm up high.

Bree looked closely at the worm. "Hi, Wormy," she said. It tickled when it crawled. She brushed it gently with her finger and—oh!

It made a curly Q back and forth. It tickled so much, she almost dropped it. "Be careful, Wormy. I don't want you to get hurt."

"Can I see your worm?"

Bree looked up. It was Johanna. She knelt down next to Bree and said, "I like worms too."

Bree smiled. She didn't know anyone else who liked worms.
"It's a baby worm," she said.

Johanna said, "Let's find her mommy." Bree and Johanna
began digging together.

They dug for a long time.

Finally Johanna scooped up a big worm. "Here's the mommy!" She picked up a bucket, put in the worm, and sprinkled in some soil.

Johanna tipped the bucket toward Bree. "Here's the worm house. You want to put the baby in with the mommy?"

Johanna smiled as Bree set Wormy next to the mom and said, "Let's find more." The two went back to digging, side by side.

Bree thought she was digging twice as fast with Johanna.
She hoped they would find a whole family of worms.

And they did!

Johanna found a brother worm
and a sister worm.

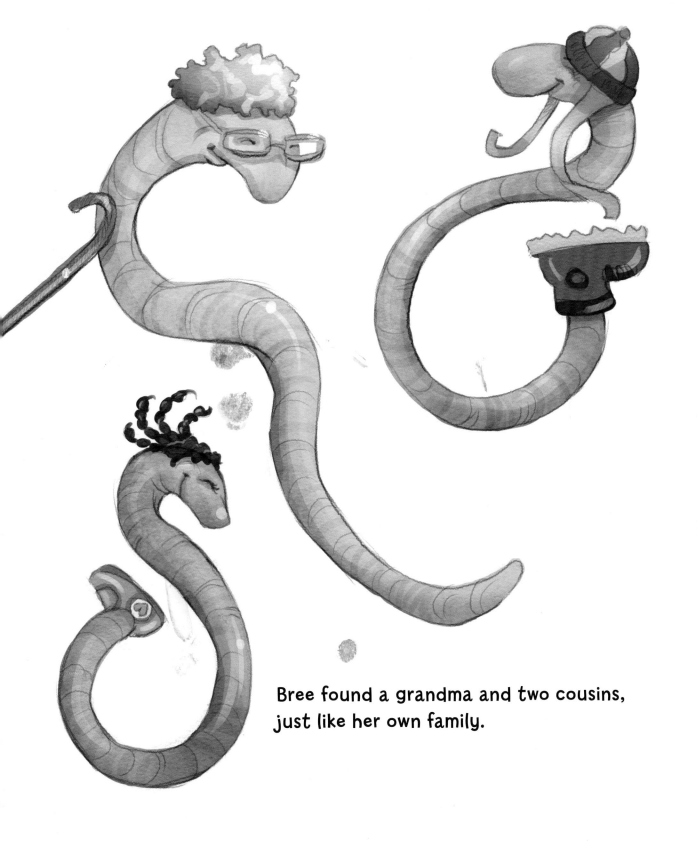

Bree found a grandma and two cousins,
just like her own family.

They put all the worms in the worm house. Bree watched the worms crawl all around.

"They love each other," she said.

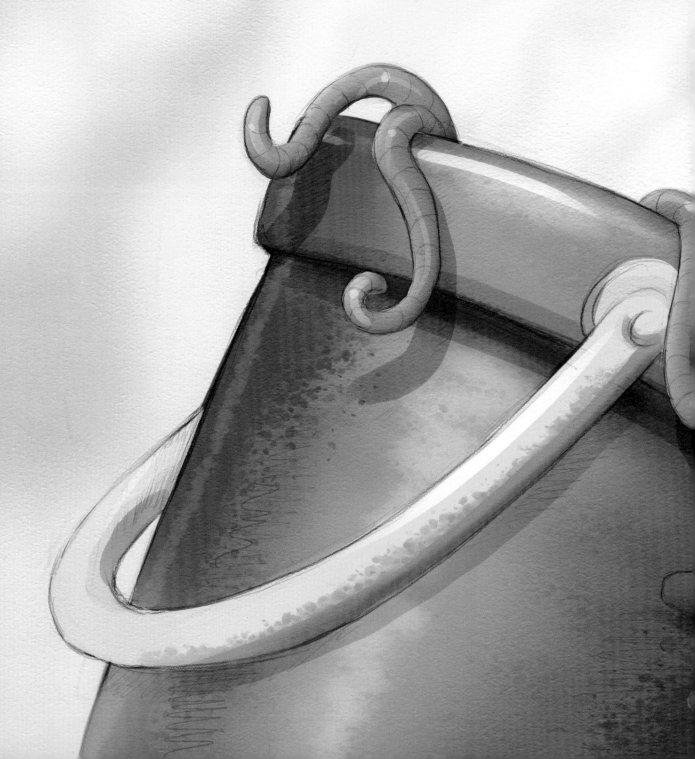

"Time for snack!" Regina called out. Johanna smiled at Bree and said, "Let's play with the worms during next outside time."

Johanna put the bucket high on a shelf. "That should keep them safe."

Bree waved. "Bye-bye, Wormy.
See you soon."

Then Johanna took Bree's hand,
and the two new friends went inside.

A Note to Readers

What does it mean to be friends with someone? Bree thinks it's fun to dig in the dirt, especially when she finds worms. Johanna likes digging for worms too. The girls discover they share the same interest and begin to become friends. Children have a variety of interests, and often several children enjoy the same things. Their friendships grow out of interests they share.

Young children need time to explore their interests and to decide for themselves who is a friend and who is not. You can help by letting children take the lead. Acknowledge that children have different styles and temperaments, which may mean that a child has a lot of friends, just one friend, or no friends. Regardless, you can help all children learn how to positively interact with peers and to expect a positive outcome from their interactions.

We hope *Bree Finds a Friend* helps children understand that common interests are one of the things that bring people together. It's fun to do things you like, especially with a friend.